Magic Ballerina™

Delphie and the Magic Ballet Shoes

Welcome to the world of Enchantia!

*I have always loved to dance. The captivating
music and wonderful stories of ballet are so
inspiring. So come with me and let's follow
Delphie on her magical adventures in
Enchantia, where the stories of dance will
take you on a very special journey.*

*p.s Turn to the back to learn a special
dance step from me...*

Special thanks to
Linda Chapman and
Katie May

First published in Great Britain by HarperCollins *Children's Books* 2008
HarperCollins *Children's Books* is a division of HarperCollins *Publishers* Ltd,
77-85 Fulham Palace Road, Hammersmith, London W6 8JB

The HarperCollins *Children's Books* website address is
www.harpercollins.co.uk

1

Text copyright © HarperCollins *Children's Books* 2008
Illustrations by Katie May
Illustrations copyright © HarperCollins *Children's Books* 2008

ISBN 978 0 00 785906 1

Printed and bound in England by
Clays Ltd, St Ives plc

Conditions of Sale
This book is sold subject to the condition that it shall not, by way of trade
or otherwise, be lent, re-sold, hired out or otherwise circulated without
the publisher's prior written consent in any form of binding or cover other
than that in which it is published and without a similar condition including
this condition being imposed on the subsequent purchaser.

FSC is a non-profit international organisation established to promote the
responsible management of the world's forests. Products carrying the FSC
label are independently certified to assure consumers that they come
from forests that are managed to meet the social, economic and
ecological needs of present and future generations.

Find out more about HarperCollins and the environment at
www.harpercollins.co.uk/green

Magic Ballerina

Delphie and the Magic Ballet Shoes

Darcey Bussell

HarperCollins *Children's Books*

To Phoebe and Zoe, as they are the inspiration behind Magic Ballerina.

Contents

Prologue

In the soft, pale light, the girl stood
with her head bent and her hands
held lightly in front of her.
There was a moment's silence and then
the first notes of the music began.
For as long as the girl could remember
music had seemed to tell her of
another world – a magical, exciting
world – that lay far, far away.
She always felt if she could just
close her eyes and lose herself,
then she would get there.
Maybe this time. As the music
swirled inside her, she swept
her arms above her head, rose on to
her toes and began to dance...

Madame Zarakova's School of Ballet

Delphie hurried home, her breath freezing in the snowy night air. The houses on either side of the road had their curtains drawn – all apart from one – a big double-fronted house with iron railings and a gate. Two stone steps led up to the door and light streamed out of the windows. As the snowflakes landed softly on Delphie's shoulders, she looked longingly at the brass plate, just as she had for the last four weeks since it had been open: *Madame Zarakova's School of Ballet.*

A car drew up outside and two girls jumped out. They were about nine – the same age as Delphie – and had their hair tied back in neat buns.

"Come on, we're going to be late!" one of them called as they ran through the gate and opened the front door. "Madame Za-Za will go mad!"

For a moment, Delphie caught sight of a long wide hallway with white walls and wooden floors before the heavy door banged shut behind them.

Delphie felt a wave of longing so strong it hurt. She wanted to be inside the ballet school about to have a dance lesson. She was ballet-mad but her parents had always put her off having lessons.

"Maybe when you're a bit older," her mum had said, kissing Delphie's long dark hair. "The nearest dance school is on the other side of town. It's too far to take you every week."

But Delphie hadn't been put off. She had borrowed books from the library and practised ballet exercises almost every day. And she danced all the time – in the house, in the garden, she wasn't even embarrassed to dance on the street! She loved the feeling of spinning, moving, jumping. It was hard to explain but, although she had never had any lessons,

inside she just felt like she knew what it was like to be a real ballerina.

And now Madame Zarakova's ballet school had opened on the very street she lived. But even that hadn't helped her. Delphie did understand. After all, money was quite tight in their house.

"I'm sorry, sweetheart," Mrs Durand, Delphie's mum, had sighed. "We just can't afford to send you there."

Standing by the railings now, Delphie could now hear the faint sounds of a piano tinkling and, through the branches, she could see light from the big windows falling into the front garden. Shivering she pulled her coat closer around her as she looked over the railings.

The music and lights seemed to be calling her nearer. Slipping through the gate, she crept over to the house, peering in through the window. The room inside was large with mirrors on each of the four walls. Eight girls, all about the same age, were holding lightly to the *barre*, a wooden pole that was fixed around the wall of the room. They were all dressed in pink leotards with a ribbon round their waists, pale socks and satin ballet shoes with ribbons crossed neatly round their ankles.

They were gracefully bending and straightening their knees out over their toes.

"*Pliés*," Delphie sighed longingly,
recognising them from one of her books.
Oh, if only she could be in there with them.

Madame Za-Za was walking around the room, talking to the girls and correcting a leg position here, an arm position there. She held her own body erect and her grey-streaked brown hair was pulled back in a bun. As Delphie watched, the girls began a different exercise, pointing their toes and sliding their legs to the back, front and side. *Battements tendu*, thought Delphie. All the girls looked good but there was one dark-haired girl who looked very graceful and seemed to find everything very easy.

Next the girls began sliding the foot that was furthest from the *barre* and lifting it off the floor, stretching out as far as they could and holding their free arm out to the side.

Delphie couldn't resist. She began to join in.

Holding on to the windowsill,
she performed the
movement in time with
the girls inside.

Sweeping her arm
and leg to the side, she
held them in perfect
position, her toe pointed
and heel raised from the
ground. They moved
quickly into practising
quick, light movements.

Madame Za-Za said something to the
girls and left the room. The class carried on
working. Feeling very happy, Delphie
continued to copy them. It was almost like
being in there.

Then, suddenly, the front
door swung open and a
voice called out. "You, girl!
What are you doing?"

Delphie jumped in shock
and swung round. She had
been concentrating so hard
on the dancing that she
hadn't heard it opening.
It was Madame Za-Za
standing on the top step,
staring at her!

Delphie froze to the spot. "I… I'm really
sorry! I just wanted to have a look."

"Come here, child!" Madame Za-Za called.

And with just a moment's hesitation,
Delphie hurried up the steps.

The Red Ballet Shoes

"Come inside, child" Madame Za-Za said. "What is your name?"

"Delphie Durand." Delphie felt tears prickling her eyes. She was sure she was about to be told off. She blinked quickly; she hated crying in front of people.

"I saw you through the window,"

Madame Za-Za said to her. "Where do you learn ballet?"

Delphie was very surprised by the question. "I… I don't go to classes," she answered. "I just read about it in books and practise at home."

"I see." Madame Za-Za looked at her for a moment. "Well, why don't you come in?"

"Come in?" Delphie echoed.

Madame Za-Za nodded. "It's cold out here and I think you would like to see around. Am I right?"

"Yes!" Delphie gasped. "I'd love to see inside."

"Come, then."

Walking in a daze, Delphie followed Madame Za-Za inside the school. They went down the warm, brightly lit corridor. "Here we have the dance studios," Madame Za-Za explained, pointing to two rooms, one on either side.

"Wow!" Delphie breathed.

Madame Za-Za looked thoughtfully at her. "Do you have any ballet shoes, child?"

"No," Delphie replied. She always just danced in bare feet.

Madame Za-Za gave a small nod and

then set off down a dark corridor, opening a door at the end that led into a small storeroom. The walls were covered with shelves piled high with boxes, dusty books, ballet costumes and what looked like a chest full of new ballet leotards and socks.

Madame Za-Za went into the room and took an old, battered box down from a high shelf.

As Delphie watched, Madame Za-Za opened the lid to reveal a pair of old red leather ballet shoes with red ribbons, nestling among yellowing tissue paper. The leather was slightly crinkly, the insides of the shoes a deep cream. They were worn and slightly shabby but as Delphie looked at them, she felt a sudden urge to reach into the box.

Her feet tingled as if they wanted to try them on.

Unable to stop herself she touched the soft red leather and then realising what she was doing, she pulled her hand back.

She looked up to see Madame Za-Za studying her face, her expression unreadable.

"Do you like them?" Madame Za-Za asked.
"Oh yes," Delphie breathed. The ballet
shoes might be old but
they were beautiful.
"Would you like
to borrow them,
child?" Madame
Za-Za asked gently.

"Borrow them!" Delphie stared in
surprise. "But why would you lend them to
me? I don't even come here to classes."

"If you like you can come back tomorrow
and join in with the class you were watching,"
Madame Za-Za said.

Delphie could hardly believe her ears.
"But… but… well, I'd love to but Mum and
Dad can't afford for me to have lessons." She

blushed as she admitted the truth.

Madame Za-Za waved her hand dismissively. "Money does not matter. Just come tomorrow as I ask." Her eyes met Delphie's. "I will teach you for free."

Delphie's mind spun.

"Go home now and tell your parents what I have said. They may ring me if they have any questions." Madame Za-Za gave her the box with the ballet shoes and then turned and took a brand-new pink leotard and socks out of the chest near the door. "Bring these clothes and the shoes to wear tomorrow."

Delphie looked down at the box in her arms. "What if the shoes don't fit me?"

Madame Za-Za gave a mysterious smile. "Oh, I don't think there will be a problem with that. I think you will find them the perfect size. They have been waiting for the right person to come along and something tells me you might be that person."

Her eyes stared deep into Delphie's. "They are very special shoes, Delphie. I hope one day you find out just how special they are." Suddenly her tone became brisker. "Now, I must return to class. I will see you tomorrow, ready and changed for half past four sharp."

"Thank you!" Delphie gasped.

Almost before she knew it, she was following Madame Za-Za back down the corridor and then she was back outside in the snow again. But Delphie didn't feel cold. Excitement raced through her as she hugged the shoes to her chest. She rushed home to tell her Mum. She was going to start ballet classes tomorrow. She couldn't wait!

The Ballet Class

Delphie could hardly concentrate in school at all the next day. All she could think about was her first ballet lesson. She was at Madame Za-Za's school by four o'clock and had changed twenty minutes before the class was due to start.

As Delphie tied her long hair back into a bun, she looked at herself in the mirror and couldn't stop grinning. She looked just like

the girls she had been watching the day before. Well, apart from the fact that her shoes were red instead of pale pink but Delphie didn't care about that. They were beautifully soft and they fitted her perfectly, just as Madame Za-Za had said they would.

Other girls started to arrive. The two who Delphie had seen running into the ballet school the day before were the first to get there. "Who are you?" one of them asked curiously.

"I'm Delphie," Delphie replied.

"Are you just starting lessons here?" the other girl asked.

Delphie nodded.

"Well, I'm Poppy," the first girl said.
"And this is Lola."

"Hiya Delphie," Lola smiled.

Other girls started to pile in. They were just as friendly and at half past four they all went into the dance studio where Madame Za-Za was waiting for them.

They began with *pliés* at the *barre*. Delphie concentrated hard, trying to remember everything she had read in her books.

As she followed Madame Za-Za's instructions, she felt herself relax and soon it was just as if she was practising in her bedroom at home but a hundred times better because she was in a real ballet class.

Madame Za-Za kept telling them all to keep their heads up and to smile but Delphie didn't find that difficult at all.

The girls moved from the *barre* to working

in the centre of the room. They went
through the same exercises again and then
practised arm movements, different poses
and turns called pirouettes.

As they neared the end of the class,
Madame Za-Za explained to Delphie that
the class had been learning a dance from a
ballet called *The Nutcracker*.

Delphie had read about *The Nutcracker* –
a girl called Clara was given a nutcracker
who looked like a soldier as a Christmas
present by her uncle. Clara loved her new
toy so much that she crept downstairs
when everyone was in bed and danced
with him before falling asleep.

"I think you had better just watch this bit
of the class, Delphie," Madame Za-Za said

to her. "The others have been learning the dance for a while now."

Delphie sat, feeling nervous, as the other eight girls took it in turns to hold a wooden doll which looked like a toy soldier and dance Clara's dance. The dark-haired girl, who Delphie had found out was called

Sukie, was the last to go. She moved very gracefully and didn't wobble on any of the positions she held. Her turns were easy and smooth

35

and her arms and head always seemed to be held perfectly in position. But even so there was something that wasn't quite right. *What is it?* Delphie wondered.

Madame Za-Za was watching from near the piano. As Sukie finished and smiled, Madame Za-Za walked forward, shaking

her head. "No, Sukie, Your hands, your arms, your placing were all good, but you are supposed to love the doll you are holding. I did not believe that when I watched you."

Delphie realised she knew exactly what Madame Za-Za meant. Although Sukie's dancing had looked wonderful, she hadn't made Delphie feel like she was really watching Clara.

Madame Za-Za turned to all the girls. "Ballet is about much more than just dancing – the real magic comes from telling a story and making the audience believe in that story." Her eyes looked straight into Delphie's. "Never forget that – always believe in it."

Delphie felt a longing to do the dance herself. She wanted to be up there, wanted Madame Za-Za to be watching her, but it was too late – it was the end of the class.

As soon as she had got changed, Delphie ran all the way home. She couldn't wait to tell her parents about it. This had been the best day of her life!

That night, when Delphie went to bed, she relived every moment of the class. *I'll have to learn the dance the others were doing*, she thought, picking up a book that was lying on her bedside table which told all the stories from the ballet.

Delphie turned to the chapter on *The Nutcracker*. She wanted to know what happened after Clara's dance. She read how, in the story, Clara dreams that the Nutcracker has come to life! Then the evil King Rat, with his army of mice, tries to fight the Nutcracker. Clara helps to defeat King Rat by throwing her slipper at his head, which knocks him out. Then the

Nutcracker changes into a handsome prince and takes Clara on a magical journey to the Land of Snow and the Land of Sweets. She meets the Sugar Plum Fairy and lots of other amazing characters like the snowflakes and Jack Frost, the Rose Fairy and the Arabian dancers.

Delphie sighed happily as she read the end of the story. Turning off the light she snuggled down in bed, imagining herself dancing Clara's dance, when suddenly she heard a faint tinkling sound and some faraway music. What was that?

She listened hard. There it was again. She sat up in bed.

The red ballet shoes were glittering and sparkling in the dark!

A Magical Land

Delphie stared at the twinkling shoes and then leapt out of bed. She was about to run out of the room to get her mum when Madame Za-Za' s voice came back to her: *They are special shoes, Delphie. I hope that one day you will find out just how special they are.*

Something seemed to be telling Delphie

to stay – not to go. She reached out and
touched the shoes. Her fingers seemed to
spark with a tiny electric shock and suddenly
she felt as if she just had to put them on.

She picked up the left shoe. As she slipped it on, her foot felt light and sparkly. She put the other shoe on and as she tied the ribbons, the tingling spread through her whole body. Delphie stood up and then gasped as suddenly the shoes began to make her pirouette round and round…

Delphie whirled, her bedroom blurring into a sparkling haze of colours. She cried out. *What was happening?*

Then the colours faded and she found herself on a seat. She looked around in astonishment. She was in a large empty theatre. In front of her there was an enormous stage with red curtains, shut tight. The lights began to go down and before Delphie's eyes, the curtains rose.

A scene of a village street appeared with
a large mountain behind it. On the slope
of the mountain, a dark castle was painted.
Feeling sure that she must be dreaming,
Delphie looked at the stage. A fairy in a
pale lilac tutu was sitting on a tree stump,
her hands covering her face.

Behind her there were dancers dressed as multi-coloured flowers, two people in Russian costumes, a girl in a long red Spanish dress and a clown. Delphie wondered if this was the beginning of some sort of show, but as she looked more closely, she realised that the fairy was crying.

Delphie got to her feet and went down the aisle that led up to the stage. "Hello!" she called. Her voice sounded loud in the silence of the theatre.

The fairy jumped in surprise. "Who are you?"

"My name's Delphie," Delphie replied. "Who are you?"

"I'm the Sugar Plum Fairy," she said.

"You mean you're dancing the part of the Sugar Plum Fairy in *The Nutcracker*," Delphie said, feeling confused.

"No, I really am the Sugar Plum Fairy." The ballerina stood up, her sparkling tutu catching the lights on the stage. "People call me Sugar for short. This is the entrance to the Land of Enchantia – the land where the characters from all the different ballets live." She looked curiously at Delphie. "Where have you come from?"

"From… from my bedroom," Delphie stammered. "My ballet shoes started to sparkle and so I put them on and I ended up here."

"You've got the magic ballet shoes!" Sugar breathed. "I've heard about those.

Every so often they are given to someone who really loves ballet and they bring them to Enchantia. It happens whenever there's a problem here."

Delphie stared at her. "Madame Za-Za – the person who gave them to me – said they were special. She must have meant they were magic." Delphie's eyes widened and she looked around wonderingly. "So this is all real. It's not a dream." She remembered something the Sugar Plum Fairy had just said. "You said the shoes work when there's a problem."

Sugar nodded. "Yes, and we have a very big problem right now. The people in Enchantia usually live happily together and

dance all day. But not any more." Her blue eyes welled up with tears. "Evil King Rat has stopped everyone from dancing."

"King Rat?" Delphie echoed, thinking back to the villain of the ballet she'd been reading about before she went to bed.

Sugar nodded sadly. "He hates dancing. He's captured the Nutcracker and turned him into a wooden toy. Without the

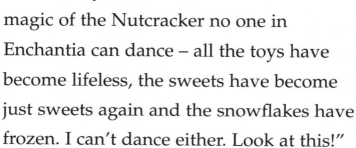

magic of the Nutcracker no one in Enchantia can dance – all the toys have become lifeless, the sweets have become just sweets again and the snowflakes have frozen. I can't dance either. Look at this!"

She stood up and with a
graceful lift of her arms,
she rose on to her
pointes but she only
managed to dance
three steps forwards
before she wobbled
over. "The magic of
the dance has gone.
The only way to stop
King Rat is to free the
Nutcracker and bring him back to life again
but King Rat is keeping him prisoner in his
castle and everyone's too scared to go there."

Delphie thought how awful it would be
not to be able to dance. "I'll help you," she
said eagerly.

"It could be very dangerous," Sugar warned. "The castle is guarded by King Rat's army of mice. They're big and carry swords and are very fierce."

"I don't care," said Delphie bravely. "I want to help you free the Nutcracker!"

"Oh, thank you!" Sugar grabbed Delphie's hands. "Thank you so much!"

"So, how do we get to the castle?" Delphie asked.

Sugar smiled. "By magic of course!"

Off to the Castle!

Sugar pulled a silver wand out of a pocket in her tutu and waved it in the air. Purple sparks flew out and swirled round them in a haze. Delphie felt herself pirouetting round three times in the air before she landed on her feet and the sparkles cleared.

Delphie gasped. They were no longer on the stage but standing in a wood with

fallen branches and leaves beneath their feet. The air smelt horrid – of rotten fruit and old food.

"That's King Rat's castle," whispered Sugar pointing through the trees. Delphie could see a dark shape looming ahead of them, its stone turrets silhouetted against the sky.

Two mice, a bit taller than Delphie, were
guarding the big wooden door that led into
the castle. They were standing on their back
legs and had swords slung through leather
belts. Their eyes were beady and
their snouts were long.

"What's that horrid smell?"
Delphie whispered back.

"King Rat gets his mice to
bring great piles of rubbish here so he can
rummage around in it and eat it to his
heart's content. He loves it."

Sugar waved her wand. There was a
tinkle of music and two sugar-coated plums
appeared in her hand. "These should help
take the smell away. Put one in your
pocket." She handed one to Delphie.

Delphie breathed in a
wave of sweetness –
icing sugar, candyfloss,
fresh plums and
peaches. "That's much

better!" She slipped the sugarplum into
her pocket and looked around. "How are
we going to get into the castle to rescue
the Nutcracker?"

"I don't know," said Sugar. "I can use
my magic to travel around Enchantia,
but I can't use it to get inside King Rat's
castle. His powers are much stronger
than mine."

Delphie crept forward to the edge of the
trees. How were they going to get in?

Suddenly both mice sniffed the air.

"Sugarplums!" said the mouse on the left who was tall and thin with very pointed teeth. "I smell sugarplums!"

"Me too," said the other mouse, who was smaller and fatter with tiny eyes.

They scented the air. "It smells like they're this way!" said the

thin mouse, starting to walk away from the castle and towards the trees where Delphie and Sugar were hiding.

"They're coming over here!" Delphie whispered in alarm.

Sugar looked dismayed. "I forgot that all of King Rat's mice love sugarplums! I'd better magic us away!"

But Delphie had noticed something. With the mice walking away from the castle, the door was unguarded. An idea popped into her mind. If they could just get the mice into the trees and properly away from the door...

"Wait!" she hissed as Sugar lifted her wand. "This could be our chance to get into the castle! Can you get me some more sugarplums – and fast!"

"It's too dangerous!" said Sugar as the mice approached the trees.

"Please!" Delphie begged.

Sugar hesitated and then pointed her wand at the ground. With a faint tinkle, a pile of sugarplums appeared.

Delphie picked up as many as she could. "Quick! Let's make a trail leading away from the castle!"

Sugar grabbed the remaining plums and they hurried through the trees. They placed one of the plums near the entrance to the wood and then another and then another, all leading down the hill away from the castle. Delphie glanced round. Already she could hear the mice crashing through the woods! Sugar put the last plum where the wood ended in a steep bank that led into a shallow but fast-flowing stream.

Delphie suddenly had an idea of how to get the mice really out of the way. "If only we had some string."

"How about some ballet ribbon!" Sugar waved her wand and a big roll of pink ribbon appeared in her hand. "What do you want it for?"

"To hopefully get two mice very wet!" grinned Delphie.

She raced to the bank and tied one end of the ribbon round a tree on the left side

and the other end round a tree on the right side. Then she smiled and grabbed Sugar's hand. "Come on! They mustn't see us."

She pulled Sugar back to the edge of the woods where there was a big bramble bush to hide behind, just as the smaller mouse burst into sight.

"I found the sugarplum!" he exclaimed, snatching it up.

The tall one appeared just behind him. "There's another!" he cried, pouncing on the pale fruit. "And look! There's more of them!"

Peeping out from behind the bush, Delphie and Sugar watched as the mice began to run down the hill, scooping up the sweet plums and squabbling over them.

"I saw that one first!"

"I want it!"

"No! I want it!"

The two mice were so busy jostling and pushing each other that they didn't see the ribbon stretched across the path until they both tripped over it.

"Whoa!" shouted the mice grabbing hold of each other as they crashed to the ground. Over and over they tumbled down the bank until with two very loud splashes they fell, still shouting, into the stream.

Sugar gasped, looking half-shocked and half-delighted. "Oh, Delphie! You've made them so wet!"

Delphie grinned. "Maybe that'll teach them not to be so greedy in future. Come on! Let's get inside the castle while they're busy drying off."

They raced towards the entrance. The wooden door had a huge metal handle in the shape of a rat's head. Delphie turned it and the door opened. On the other side there was an enormous empty hall with a stone fireplace. Above it there was a framed picture of a black rat with a crown on his head and a red cloak.

On the far side of the room were two towers of boxes, piled almost up to the ceiling with the words GLUE printed on the sides of them.

"Look!" Sugar pointed to a table just in front of the boxes. Standing on top of it was a small painted wooden figure. He looked like a soldier wearing a red jacket with brass buttons, black trousers and boots and a sword in his belt.

"It's the Nutcracker!" Delphie said, running over and picking the figure up.

But then she heard a noise. It sounded like footsteps marching towards the door on the left.

"Get back in the hall!" came a voice outside the door. "You know King Rat said the Nutcracker wasn't to be left on his own! Call yourself a soldier! Coming to me with poppycock stories about smelling sugarplums through the windows!"

"But I did, Sarge. I really did. I…"

"GET BACK IN THERE!"

"Quick!" Delphie gasped to Sugar. "There's someone coming! We've got to hide!"

Dancing Magic

Delphie ran over and turned the handle of a door at the side of the hall. It opened into a small room which seemed to be used for keeping firewood. "In here!" she gasped.

Just as they were about to go in, Sugar waved her wand at the table. There was a tinkling sound and she magicked up another Nutcracker doll. "I'll put this on the table in front of the boxes so that they won't realise the real nutcracker has gone."

Delphie and Sugar dived into the room and peeped back round the door just in time. Two mice hurried into the hall. One was dressed with boots and a sword like the mice outside had been. The other was wearing a smart waistcoat with gold buttons. He looked very relieved when he saw the fake Nutcracker on the table in front of the boxes. "Lucky for you that the Nutcracker's still here. King Rat's been ever so pleased since he turned him into a toy.

He was going to use the quick-drying glue in those boxes to stick all those horrible dancers to the ground but he doesn't have to now. No

one can dance while the Nutcracker's a prisoner here." He glowered at the other mouse. "So, stay where you are and don't let anyone past!"

The other mouse nodded and the Sergeant strode out.

Sugar looked scared. "If that mouse stays outside the door then we're trapped in here!"

"Maybe there's another way out." Delphie looked around. But there were no windows or other doors in the little room.

"If only we could bring the Nutcracker back to life, he would be able to help us fight our way out," Sugar said.

"Can't you use your magic to make him come alive again?" Delphie asked hopefully.

Sugar shook her head. "King Rat's

powers are too strong while we're inside the castle. Only really powerful magic will turn him back."

Suddenly Delphie heard Madame Za-Za's words from that afternoon echo in her head: *The real magic of the ballet comes from telling a story and making the audience believe in that story. Never forget that – always believe in it.*

Delphie remembered how Madame Za-Za had looked straight at her while she had been speaking. It had been as if she had been talking directly to her. *Never forget the story…*

Maybe she'd been trying to tell her something. Delphie began to think hard. What happened in the story of *The Nutcracker* before the toy came to life?

Of course, she realised. *Clara dances with the toy Nutcracker.* An idea grew in her head. Maybe if she danced with *this* Nutcracker he would come to life too!

Almost before the idea had formed in her mind, Delphie's feet began to tingle and in her head she heard the opening bars of the dance she had watched the girls doing that afternoon. Delphie moved forward into the opening pose. Holding her arms down low and with her left foot pointed forward in front of her, she looked down at the Nutcracker in her hands.

I'm Clara, she told herself and then she began to do the dance she had been longing to do ever since the class that afternoon.

She skipped forward with tiny steps as if she was floating across the floor. Stopping, she raised her hands, drew her right leg up against her left and stretched it out behind her, staying perfectly balanced.

She gasped. The Nutcracker's arm had started to raise and his mouth to open...

Sugar stared. "Your dance is bringing him to life! Dance some more, Delphie!"

Delphie didn't need any more urging. She moved into a pirouette, ran forward a few steps then nimbly jumped into the air. She lifted the Nutcracker high up and spun round with him, her whole body glowing and tingling with the music as in her mind she became Clara dancing with her beloved doll.

There was a bright white flash. Delphie stopped with a gasp. The Nutcracker had come to life!

"Hello, Delphie," he said, smiling down at her.

Sugar threw her arms around him. "Oh, Nutcracker! Delphie's brought you back by dancing."

The Nutcracker nodded. "The strongest magic of all." He hugged her. "And now everyone in Enchantia will be able to dance again!" He looked at Delphie. "I can't thank you enough. You must have really believed in the dance to make the magic work." He took her hand. "Thank you," he said softly.

Delphie grinned in delight.

Sugar ran to the door. "We need to get out of here then I can use my magic to take us back to the village.

"Follow me!" The Nutcracker pulled out his sword and opened the door.

Escape!

The mouse who was standing guard by the table squeaked in surprise. "It's you!" He swung round and looked at the fake Nutcracker doll. "But... but... how can it be?"

The Nutcracker smiled. "Ballet magic," he said. "Let us past!"

"Oh no you don't," said the mouse running

to stand between him and the front door.
"You aren't getting away that easily!"

With one swift movement the Nutcracker
danced forward and used his sword to flip
the sword out of the mouse's grip. It flew
into the air and landed with a clatter on the
floor. With nothing to protect him, the
mouse ran hastily backwards. "Help!
Help!" he shouted. "The Nutcracker's
escaping!"

There was the sound of running footsteps.
Then suddenly a door slammed open and a
very loud voice boomed into the room.

"What is the meaning of this?"

The mice cringed, and Delphie stared as a
haughty black rat with red eyes walked
into the room, flanked by four guards.

He was wearing a
purple cloak
trimmed with
white fur, and
he had a
golden crown
on his head.
He saw the
Nutcracker
and stopped.
"You!" he
exclaimed. "I
turned you into
a toy!"

"But now I have turned back!" cried the
Nutcracker. "And all of Enchantia will
dance again!"

"Not if I have anything to do with it!" King Rat leapt forward, swiping his sword viciously at the Nutcracker. His guards closed in as well. Bravely, the Nutcracker fought them off with strong, sweeping swipes. But he was being beaten back.

"There's too many of them for the Nutcracker to fight!" Sugar exclaimed as the king and the guards advanced with their swords. They began to back the brave Nutcracker into the corner where the piles of boxes marked GLUE were stacked. He knocked against them and they wobbled precariously.

Suddenly, Delphie had an idea. She pulled off one of her ballet shoes. "Stop it, King Rat!" she shouted.

King Rat swung round. "Who are you?"

"Delphie!" She lifted the shoe up and hurled it at him.

King Rat ducked. "That's the oldest trick in the book!" he said as the shoe hit the boxes behind him. "Missed!"

"Oh no I didn't!" exclaimed Delphie as the pile of boxes began to sway.

The Nutcracker leapt nimbly out of the way, grabbing Delphie's ballet shoe from the floor as he did so, but King Rat was too busy laughing at Delphie to notice the boxes. "You missed! You did! You…"

His voice was drowned out as the boxes toppled over. They crashed down, jars of glue raining on his head. "Ow! Ooh! Ow!" he yelled.

The guards cried and shouted too. The jars smashed into each other as they fell, cracking open and covering King Rat and his soldiers in quick-drying white glue.

King Rat pointed at Delphie, glue dripping down over his face and off his ears and whiskers. "Why you... you...!"

But though he tried to run towards her, his feet were stuck fast!

"Come on," gasped Delphie, turning to Sugar and the Nutcracker. "Let's get out of here!"

And quickly they raced out of the castle and back to the woods.

"That was brilliant, Delphie!" exclaimed Sugar.

"Fantastic!" said the Nutcracker, giving her her shoe back.

"We're free – that's the main thing," Delphie grinned as she put it back on.

"And Enchantia should be returned to normal," said Sugar. "Come on, let's use my magic to get away from here and see what's happening!"

She waved her wand. Delphie found herself spinning round three times. When they landed she saw that they were in the village that she had seen painted on the scenery in the theatre. The streets were full of characters from the ballet – toys, enormous sweets, dancers dressed up

as bright flowers, two Spanish dancers and a beautiful fairy in a rose-pink dress dancing on her pointes.

Music was flooding magically through the air. Sugar grabbed Delphie's hands. "Let's dance!"

Holding lightly on to the Sugar Plum Fairy's hands, Delphie felt herself being swept up in the music – she didn't have to stop to think what steps she was going to do. As Sugar rose on to her pointes, Delphie let the music guide her – she skimmed across the ground with tiny steps, and jumped into the air, her arms outstretched, her toes pointed. She landed softly and then, with perfect balance, she stretched one leg out behind her. Delphie couldn't believe

how graceful she felt! It seemed like the music was flowing through her as she and Sugar ran forward together and pirouetted. The Nutcracker leapt in front of them, turning into a handsome prince as he landed. His

glittering costume perfectly matched
Sugar's. Delphie gasped as he swept the
Sugar Plum Fairy up in his arms and lifted
her high into the air. He turned and placed
her lightly down. Holding on to his hand
she turned round on the tip of her toe. All
around them the other characters danced
too – the flowers waltzed, the snowflakes
twirled, the Spanish dancers swung their
tiered red skirts and the Russian dancers
linked arms. There was colour and
movement everywhere. The Nutcracker
and Sugar came to a stop, their cheeks
flushed, their eyes shining.

"It is almost time for you to go home,
Delphie," the Nutcracker Prince said. "We
can't thank you enough."

A thought struck Delphie. "I hope Mum and Dad don't wonder where I've gone!"

"Do not worry, time is different in our world and yours," said the Nutcracker. "When you get back you will find that it will be as if no time has passed at all."

Delphie felt relieved but also sad as she looked around at the enchanted world. "I don't want to leave here."

Sugar smiled at her. "You'll come back. You have the magic ballet shoes. Whenever we need you they will sparkle. If you put them on they will bring you to Enchantia again." She danced over and kissed Delphie on both cheeks, then she took out her wand. "This is to take home to remind you of us," she said, waving sparkles in the air.

Delphie gasped as a beautiful white tutu appeared in her hand. "Goodbye – and thank you," Sugar said. "Send my regards to Madame Za-Za." And with that she waved her wand over Delphie's head.

"Goodbye!" Delphie cried as the air around her swirled with colour and she began to pirouette round and round… till suddenly, she landed with a bump…

Home Again

She was back in her bedroom sitting on her bed with a beautiful white tutu lying next to her.

Could her mother have put it there?

"Perhaps it was real after all," she whispered, her head spinning as she thought about everything that had just happened. She looked down at the ballet

shoes on her feet and remembered Madame Za-Za's words: *They are very special shoes, Delphie. I hope one day you find out just how special they are…*

Delphie could hardly believe it. As she began to unlace the ribbons she thought about her ballet lessons. After her adventures in Enchantia, she was even more determined to practise really hard and get as good at ballet as she could. *After all, the better I am, the more I should be able to help in Enchantia,* she realised.

Delphie stood up and put the tutu and the shoes carefully on her bedside table. When would she next go to Enchantia and what would she have to do? She remembered what the Sugar Plum Fairy

had said: *You have the magic ballet shoes.*
Whenever we need you they will sparkle and
if you put them on they will bring you to
Enchantia.

Delphie hugged her arms around herself.
She might not know when it was going to
happen or for what she might be needed
but if the shoes glowed again, she would be
there to help in whatever way she could!

*Tiptoe over the page to learn
a special dance step...*

Darcey's Magical Masterclass

Ballet Positions

Now it's your turn. Have fun!

Prepare

Put your heels together
with toes pointing outwards.
Make an oval shape with
your arms.

First position

Now move your arms upwards so
that your hands are in line with
your belly button.

Second Position
Move your feet to
hips-width apart,
and open your arms.

Third position
Move your right foot
so that the heel touches the
middle of your left foot; Sweep
your left arm in front of you.

Fourth position
Slide your right foot forwards
and lift your left arm so it is
almost over your head.

Fifth position
Now bring both your
arms over your head.

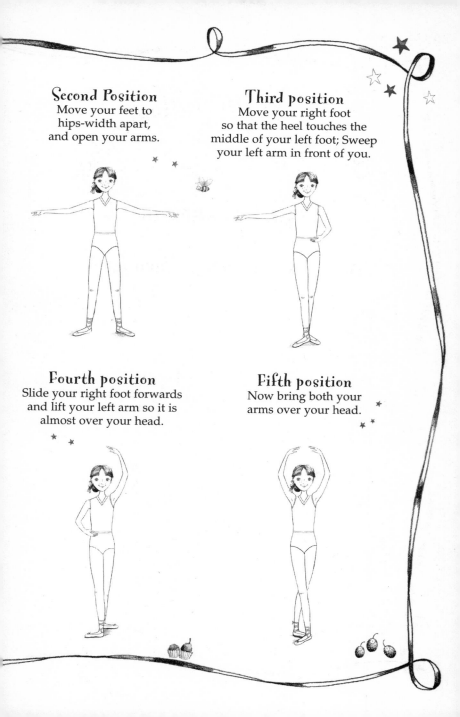

King Rat is up to his old tricks and has
cast a spell over all of Enchantia; can
Delphie help her friends before it's too late?

**Read on for a sneak preview
of book two...**

Delphie landed with a bump to find herself in the same darkened theatre only this time the air was very cold. She jumped up eagerly and then caught her breath. It was all so different. The first time she had been here there had been light and colour. The scenery had shown mountains, fields and a village, as well as King Rat's castle, and there had been lots of characters on the stage even though they had all been asleep.

But now the background scenery was just painted white and the stage was empty. The floor was covered in a thick blanket of snow. There were bare trees on the stage, their branches covered in icicles.

Delphie walked hesitantly towards the stage. "Sugar?" Her voice echoed through the empty theatre. She didn't like this. There was a feeling in the air as if something was horribly wrong.

"Sugar!" she called uneasily. "Where are you?..."

°⊙.*.☆:⊙.*.☆:⊙.*.☆.⊙.*.°

Darcey Bussell

Buy more great Magic Ballerina books direct from HarperCollins
at 10% off recommended retail price.
FREE postage and packing in the UK.

Delphie and the Magic Ballet Shoes	ISBN 978 000728607 2
Delphie and the Magic Spell	ISBN 978 000728608 9
Delphie and the Masked Ball	ISBN 978 000728610 2
Delphie and the Glass Slippers	ISBN 978 0007286 17 1
Delphie and the Fairy Godmother	ISBN 978 000728611 9
Delphie and the Birthday Show	ISBN 978 000728612 6

All priced at £3.99

To purchase by Visa/Mastercard/Switch simply call
08707871724 or fax on **08707871725**

To pay by cheque, send a copy of this form with a cheque made payable to
'HarperCollins Publishers' to: Mail Order Dept. (Ref: BOB4),
HarperCollins Publishers, Westerhill Road, Bishopbriggs, G64 2QT,
making sure to include your full name, postal address and phone number.

From time to time HarperCollins may wish to use your personal data
to send you details of other HarperCollins publications and offers.
If you wish to receive information on other HarperCollins publications
and offers please tick this box ☐

Do not send cash or currency. Prices correct at time of press.
Prices and availability are subject to change without notice.
Delivery overseas and to Ireland incurs a £2 per book postage and packing charge.